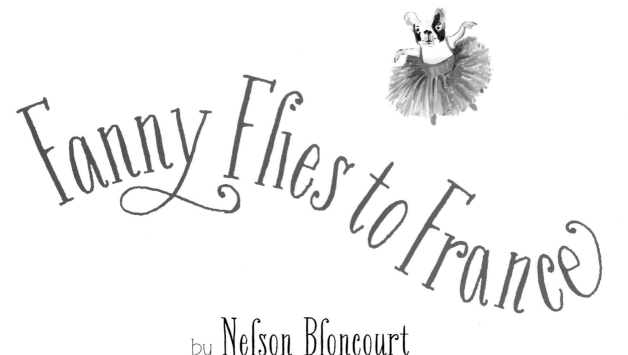

Fanny Flies to France

by Nelson Bloncourt

illustrated by Nikita Polyansky

First published in 2019 by

Glitterati Editions
311 West 43 Street, 12th Floor
New York, New York 10036

www.GlitteratiEditions.com
media@GlitteratiEditions

To all animals everywhere
for the extraordinary way they love,
the teachings they bring, and the gifts they give.
May every one of us humans commit ourselves
to their care and well-being.
–NB

To John and Julia Sneden
–NP

First edition, 2019

Library of Congress Cataloging-in-Publication data
is available from the publisher

Hardcover edition
ISBN: 978-1-943876-49-5

Printed and bound in China

10 9 8 7 6 5 4 3 2 1

In the blue, blue San Francisco sky...

...a pelican soars above Fanny. He swoops down and drops a scroll by her feet, and with a wink of his eye, he flies away.

Fanny looks to see that Dad is still napping in the hammock and quickly unties the ribbon.

Dear Miss Fanny,

Your flying show was such a wonderful addition to our circus that I want to invite you to Paris—the City of Lights!—to the annual gathering of circuses: La Grande Festival des Cirques where all of the world's magical circuses gather to meet, celebrate, and perform. Be at our tent next Sunday at noon, we will be waiting for you.

Au revoir!

Big hug and tender growl,

Leonardo

Fanny's heart leaps.

France is my family's homeland!
I must go. But how can I get away
without worrying Dad?

On Sunday morning, Fanny pretends to be asleep when her dad approaches her bed.

He pats her head. "Little girl, it looks like you want to sleep. I will be back by dinnertime."

When Fanny hears the door close, she runs to the garden, ready to fly. Her ears flap with excitement, and she is in the air.

Soon Fanny sees a blue striped tent. She lands and notices a lot of hustle and bustle. Leonardo runs over and sweeps her off of her feet with a hug.

"Miss Fanny, you made it!" says Leonardo.
"Your costume is packed and we are ready to fly."

"Fly to France?" asks Fanny. "I can't fly that far!"

"Do not worry, Miss Fanny, we all fly together.
Let's go inside the tent and you will see."

Fanny nervously walks into the tent.
She notices many of the performers she
had met before, including Frankie—the
sweet, brindle French bulldog she shared
the trapeze with—and whom she has
thought about often.

From center ring Leonardo calls, "Troupe! Attention s'il vous plaît. Attention, please. The magic floor has been laid. Everyone is now inside. We are ready to fly."

Just then the entire tent lifts into the air, rising high
above the ground, flying east across the country.
Musicians start to play.

Frankie appears before Fanny, "Want to dance?" he asks.
Her heart flutters as do her ears, and in an instant she is up
off the ground, spinning in the air. "Come fly," she says.

He takes her paws, and brings her down. "Come dance," he says. As
they dance Fanny looks at Frankie. "Why don't you fly?" she asks.
"Can't all Frenchies fly?"

"I've tried and tried," he says, "but I always fall."

"I also fell at first," says Fanny. "Do you really want to fly?"

He nods.

"Well then, I shall teach you," says Fanny.

"Now Frankie," says Fanny, "to fly, think of wonderful things. Walks in the park, delicious treats, naps, whatever makes you happy. Fill your heart with those thoughts and imagine your ears lifting you off the ground."

Frankie closes his eyes and thinks really hard about
long belly rubs, looking out the car window as the
wind blows, and his favorite bone. He tries to lift
off, but he falls. Again and again he tries.
Again and again he falls. Fanny offers
Frankie her paw. "We'll keep working on it.
You *can* do it."

The lesson is interrupted when
Leonardo calls, "We will soon
be landing!"

Fanny and Frankie run to the
open flap of the tent.

Frankie points. "That's Mont-Saint-Michel. It's an
old village, and on the top is an abbey.
They have the best buttery, sweet biscuits."
Fanny smiles hoping she might taste one.

"And that's Le Port de Havre," says Frankie.

"I know that name," says Fanny. "Do you know the story?"
Frankie shakes his head. "That's where our forefathers arrived
from England. British sailors often brought French bulldogs on
their ships as travel companions and they soon became the most
beloved dog breed of noble French ladies."

"Look," says Frankie.

"Paris!" yells Fanny.

"There's Versailles, and Fontainebleau!" Frankie points out.
And there's the Champs-Élysées and the Arc de Triomphe, where beautifully dressed people stroll and sit at cafes and eat one of my favorite treats: frites!"

All of a sudden the tent slows and begins its descent. When it lands, everyone cheers.

"Miss Fanny," Frankie says. "Welcome to our homeland!"

Fanny looks out to see that they are on a great
lawn just below the Eiffel Tower.

"Wow, I had no idea there were so many magic circuses. Are they all just like our troupe?"

"Come with me," says Frankie.

"But what about our flying lessons?" says Fanny. "They can wait," says Frankie.

Frankie leads Fanny between tents.
Some performances are already underway.
They stop now and again to watch an act.
"It's incredible," says Fanny.

Then they reach a small, tent with a
banner that reads:

"LA FÊTE FRENCHIE."

"What does that mean, Frankie?"

"It means 'The Frenchie Jubilee," says Frankie.

As they step inside Fanny sees that all the performers are French bulldogs and many of them are flying!

Someone taps Fanny on her shoulder. "Fanny, is that you?"
She turns around. It's Spanky, her neighbor from San Francisco.

"What are you doing here?" she asks.

Frenchie

But rather than answer her, he takes her paw and flying, leads her to the other side of the tent. Frankie walks over to join them.

They approach an old, grey French bulldog wearing a monocle. "Monsieur Gaston," says Spanky. "I want you to meet a dear friend of mine from home,- Fanny."

All of a sudden Monsieur Gaston hugs Fanny. "Ma belle, ma petite belle!-a friend of Spanky's is my friend as well!" He rocks her in his arms.

"I am Monsieur Gaston, master here at La Fête. Are you a performer?" he asks.

"I am here to perform in Leonardo's troupe. I am:
Fanny, The Flying Frenchie!" she says proudly and does
a loop-de-loop.

Monsieur Gaston smiles, "Ah, Leonardo. A great ringmaster,
indeed." Then Monsieur Gaston turns to Frankie. "And you,
petit garçon, do you fly in Leonardo's troupe as well?"

Shyly, Frankie says, "I am a trapeze artist."

"Do you not fly?" asks Monsieur Gaston.

Frankie looks down.

"Frankie is still learning to fly," offers Fanny.

"Maybe I can help," says Monsieur Gaston.
"All French bulldogs should enjoy flying.
Show me what you can do."

Frankie closes his eyes and flaps his ears as hard as he can. He lifts off. But in an instant is a heap on the ground.

"I told you I can't do it!" shouts Frankie, and runs out of the tent.

"Come back!" yells Fanny.

"Don't worry, ma belle," Monsieur Gaston says, "Trust me, Frankie will fly when he learns to keep love in his heart. It is there where the magic lives."

Fanny nods. *Now* she remembers.

When Fanny arrives at their tent in search of Frankie,
Leonardo scolds, "Where have you been?
The show is about to begin."

The music starts to play. Fanny looks around. She sees
Monsieur Gaston and Spanky enter the tent. Then she spots
Frankie at the foot of his platform.

Leonardo announces:

"Introducing Fanny,
the Flying Frenchie!"

Fanny soars through the air. Frankie watches Fanny for a moment then climbs the rope ladder to his trapeze platform.

Fanny lands next to Frankie on the platform.

"Wait!" shouts Fanny. She lands next to Frankie. "I forgot the most important part: Think love. That is how I discovered I could fly. I thought about my mother and my love for her."Fanny takes Frankie's paws in hers and says, "Remember, just think love to fly. Think love then let go of the bar. You will fly."

Frankie smiles at Fanny. He takes a deep breath, holds the bar, and jumps from the platform. He swings back and forth. Back and forth. Then, all of a sudden, he lets go. His big ears flutter. He wobbles.

"Think love," yells Fanny.

"Think love and fly!"

Frankie flaps his ears more and more.
"Frankie you're flying!" calls Fanny. They spin and make
loop-di-loops as the crowd cheers.

Then Frankie flies towards
Fanny and in midair, gives her a big
kiss on her cheek.

After the show Frankie asks, "Do you know what I thought
of just before I let go of the bar?"

Fanny shakes her head.

"I thought of you," says Frankie.

Fanny's heart soars. "When we leave," says Fanny,
"will you fly home with me...to meet my dad?"

"Yes," he replies, "But first
lets see Paris!"

That evening, Fanny looks out at the
full moon, marvels over the
land of her ancestors and says,
"Let's fly together, to go
eat some frites!"